NORTHUMBERLAND FOLK TALES

retold by

ROSALIND KERVEN

First published in the UK by Talking Stone 2005

Reprinted 2007

Text copyright © Rosalind Kerven 2005
Illustrations copyright © Yvonne Gilbert 2005

Talking Stone
Swindonburn Cottage West, Sharperton
Morpeth, Northumberland, NE65 7AP

ISBN: 978-0-9537454-2-5

Printed and bound in England by Antony Rowe Ltd, Chippenham, Wiltshire

CONTENTS

DRAGON CASTLE

At Bamburgh, by the sea, there looms a dark rock. On this rock there stands a castle. And in that castle there once lived a mighty king.

This king had a daughter but no sons; and his wife was dead. As the years went by, he grew tired of just the girl's company by the fireside, and he longed to marry again. So he rode out through his realm, searching high and low for a woman fine enough to be his new queen.

At length he found a highborn lady who was beautiful, quick-witted and skilled in the charms of love. She accepted the king's marriage proposal eagerly - too eagerly in the eyes of some. Within days they were celebrating their wedding. Then the new queen took her throne beside the king.

The king was ecstatically happy. For when the queen poured out his wine each night, she always laced it with love potion. But the rest of the court found the queen domineering and hardhearted: they all hated her. The one who hated her most was the queen's new stepdaughter, the princess.

The princess had almost grown up by then; and she too was very beautiful. Also, her grace and gentleness were widely admired. The new queen was jealous of her, and because of this she bullied her. She locked away the princess's jewellery, made her dress in cast-offs and sent her away early from the dinner table, so that the poor girl grew pallid and thin.

One day a special feast was held at the castle. All the guests who came to it had to swear an oath, praising the king and queen.

The nobles and their ladies all queued eagerly at the throne. One by one they fell to their knees and declared:

'You are the mightiest king
and the fairest lady in all the world!
I swear to honour you!'

Then the king rewarded each with an exquisite gift: a sword or a golden ring.

At length it was the turn of a handsome youth whom no-one had ever seen before. In fact, this youth was a stranger in the kingdom, and had only got into the feast by bribing the guards. He walked to the throne with a jaunty step, and his voice rang out loud and clear through the great hall as he declared:

'You are the mightiest king in all the world!
I swear to honour you!'

Then he rose and turned to walk away without claiming his gift. The king called him back with an angry shout:

'Hey there, young man, wait! Your oath is only half made.'

The youth made no effort to correct his mistake, and brazenly ignored the queen. He walked quickly to a stool in the shadows where the princess was quietly sitting. He bowed deeply to her. Then he said,

'My lady: they call me the Young Knight of the Wind, and I have travelled countless miles to attend this feast - all because of *you*. For it is true what they say. The queen is not the fairest lady in the world: you are!'

The princess blushed like a wild rose and gazed up at him in amazement. The king too looked astonished. But the queen leaped from her throne with a piercing shriek.

'Guards,' she cried, 'seize that slanderous wretch! Take him down to the beach. As soon as the tide turns to go out, throw him into a small boat with no oars and set him adrift on the sea!'

The guards seized the Young Knight of the Wind and dragged him away.

'The feast is cancelled!' proclaimed the queen. 'All of you: go home and keep your silence! If anyone dares say a word against me - you too shall be banished!'

The guests stood up and filed, quaking, from the hall. The luscious food piled on the tables was left untouched. The princess began to weep, and her father, the king, went to comfort her. But the queen slapped him away with an angry hiss.

'So, you little hussy,' the queen spat at the princess, 'what do you think of your admirer, eh?'

'He seems both brave and noble,' the princess whispered.

'Well, I can tell you for sure, he is neither,' snapped the queen. 'And what do you think of his judgement, eh? Do you *really* think you are the fairest lady in the world?'

'That isn't for me to answer,' the princess said.

'Indeed!' said the queen, 'so I shall answer it for you - not with words but with deeds.'

Behind the throne stood a table laden with treasures. The queen went to it and rummaged through them until she found a small, black glass bottle and a silver cup.

She pulled the stopper from the bottle and poured some dark liquid from it into the cup. Then she seized the princess, held the cup to her lips and forced the liquid down her throat.

The princess spluttered and gasped.

'Stop!' the king cried, running to her. He tried to snatch the bottle away, but the queen was too nimble. 'In God's name! - are you trying to poison her?'

'No,' said the queen, 'not poison. This is witchcraft.'

'Witchcraft?' the king cried in horror.

The queen gave a demonic laugh. 'Watch her,' she said, 'and you will see.'

For the vile brew was already taking effect. The princess was writhing about, stretching and squirming in agony. And as she stretched, her body began to change...

Her dress burst from her. Her smooth white skin blistered, and the blisters turned to scales. Her hair fell out. Horns budded on her head. Claws grew from her hands. She fell onto all-fours. Her body grew elongated, sprouting wings and a quivering tail.

The king turned white. At first he could not speak. Then he said hoarsely, 'Oh, you evil witch! How I curse the day that I married you! What have you done to my beloved daughter?'

'You must be even more of a fool than I thought, if you need to ask that,' the queen said softly. 'Can't you see with your own eyes? I've turned her into a dragon!'

Meanwhile, the Young Knight of the Wind had been bound, gagged and cast away on the sea. A fierce storm had blown up as soon as he was set adrift: this too was due to the queen's witchery. At first he feared he would be broken to smithereens on the rocks of the Farne Islands. But he had been born with luck on his side, and he found himself caught in a current that swept him safely past them and out to the open sea. There he drifted for several days; and at last found himself cast up on the shores of Norway.

Here the queen's spells were too far away to touch him, and he quickly recovered from his ordeal. He offered allegiance to the king of that land, and was rewarded with food, a place to sleep in his hall, weapons, armour and gold.

Months passed. The Young Knight of the Wind grew taller, stronger and even bolder. But although he thrived in his new life, he could not settle. For he still thought constantly of the princess.

He asked everywhere for news of her. At last he met a traveller, newly sailed in from Bamburgh, who told him:

'The queen has turned her stepdaughter into a loathsome, flame-breathing dragon. This dragon is causing chaos all over the kingdom! It's eating all the crops and animals so that the people are starving. Also, its fire is burning down all the houses.'

'But the king has many brave warriors in his court,' said the Young Knight of the Wind. 'Why don't they kill this dragon?'

'The king won't allow it,' said the traveller, 'for he can't forget that the dragon was once his beloved daughter. But it seems that the queen will soon overrule him, for due to her witchcraft, she now holds the king completely in her power. She has declared that she will allow the dragon to live in the castle for a year and a day. After that, she'll ignore the king's objections and will certainly have it killed.'

When the Young Knight of the Wind heard this, he knew that his time had come. He also realised that, although he was a skilled and valiant warrior, this was not enough to overcome the queen. So he hurried urgently to the cottage of an old woman who was famed in that land for her wisdom and knowledge of magic. He gave her a purse of the gold he had earned from serving the Norwegian king. Then he begged her to advise him what to do.

The old woman took the gold gratefully. She held a candle to the Young Knight of the Wind's face and studied him intently in its light.

'I can see you are honest,' she said at last, 'so I'll give you three pieces of advice.

'First: when you build a new boat to sail home in, make sure you use wood cut from a rowan tree. It's the only kind that's guaranteed to be stronger than witchcraft.

'Second: when the dragon comes at you, roaring with fire and hatred, your first thought will be to kill it to save your own life. Well, don't. Instead, remind yourself of who the dragon really is. Then

9

follow your heart.

'Third: when your deeds are done and the dragon's gone, there'll still be one more thing to do. Go to the queen, seize the sceptre from her hand and throw it into the waves. I promise you won't be sorry.'

The old woman shut her mouth abruptly and showed him to the door. The Young Knight of the Wind thanked her. Then he hurried away, chopped down a sturdy rowan tree and crafted it into a boat. As soon as it was finished, he set sail back to Bamburgh.

As he drew nearer, the sea swirled and seethed with the evil spells of the queen. An unnatural wind blew up and lashed the waves, tossing the little boat this way and that. Thunder rumbled and lightning struck the mast. But the rowan wood held fast and true, and the Young Knight of the Wind reached the beach below the castle without coming to any harm.

As he landed, a loud noise came bellowing at him and the air was filled with an acrid smell of burning. The sand shuddered beneath his feet. The next moment he was dazzled by the brightness of fire. Above him, the castle seemed to shake. Its gate opened and the dragon came slithering out.

It stood on the rocks in a billowing cloud of smoke. Then it spread its wings and soared into the air. Even the bold Young Knight of the Wind could not help cowering under its shadow.

Three times the beast circled him, then it landed before him on the beach.

The Young Knight of the Wind had never faced anything so huge, loathsome and ugly; never in any battle had he felt such fear! He was overwhelmed by desire to kill it. He gripped his sword and crept towards it, aiming the blade at the monster's heart. The dragon opened its vast mouth and belched out flames, watching him with red, bulbous eyes.

But at that moment, the wise woman's words came back to him. The Young Knight of the Wind turned his gaze from the dragon, and in his mind's eye he conjured a picture of his beloved princess. Oh, how lovely she had been before the queen bewitched her! - how gentle and graceful! With trembling hands, he forced himself to put away his sword.

He inched closer. The dragon stood stock still. The Young Knight of the Wind sweated under its fiery breath. He choked at its stench. Still closer he came. He put out his hands. He brushed his fingers against its warty scales...

...And even closer. Thinking of the princess, he put his lips to the dragon's scaly skin... and three times he kissed it.

On the third kiss, the dragon suddenly juddered away from him. Its fire fizzled out in a rush of cold air. It began to shrivel and shrink. Its skin collapsed as if its bones were crumbling. The sand gave way beneath it and the beast sank into a gaping hole.

Storm clouds rushed across the sky and blanked out the sun, then a wind sent the sand spiralling up until the Young Knight of the Wind was almost blinded. When it cleared he saw a pale figure emerging from the hole, luminous in the storm-light. Then he knew for sure that the evil spell was broken. For it was the princess!

She ran to the Young Knight of the Wind. He caught her in his arms and they embraced. As they did, a crowd of courtiers, servants, noble ladies and warriors came swarming from the castle and cheering down to the beach - and at their head there strode the king.

He was as overjoyed as the Young Knight of the Wind to see the loathsome dragon gone and the princess back in her own true shape. He offered the Young Knight the princess's hand in marriage and half his fortune too. The Young Knight was eager to accept - and so was the princess!

But before they could shake hands on it, the cheering crowd fell silent. For the evil queen had come down to the sand.

The queen raised her hands and began to mutter the words of another venomous spell. But the Young Knight of the Wind knew now that *his* will was stronger than hers. He strode up to her, snatched the sceptre from her hand as the wise woman had advised him, and hurled it into the sea.

At once the queen was devoured from inside by her own witchery. She began to spin round so fast that no eye could follow her. When the spinning finally slowed then stopped, she had gone. In her place stood an ugly, croaking toad.

And that was the end of the queen: all her powers of witchery were dead. In her toad shape she crawled away to a damp ditch. There she had to lurk, piteous and despised, living on flies and beetles, until she died.

As for the Young Knight of the Wind and the princess, they got married without delay, and very happy they were too. When the princess's father grew too old to reign any more, the Young Knight of the Wind became the new king; and everyone said that he ruled the land with great generosity and wisdom.

ONLY ME

A stone cottage stood right on the edge of nowhere, and in it there lived a widow and her young son. This boy was terribly lazy and wilful: he never did what he was told. He was especially wild at bedtime. Every night his mother worked like a slave, cooking, washing the dishes and banking up the kitchen stove. But *he* refused to help.

Then, when she pointed to the steps leading to the loft and ordered him: 'Up to bed with you, my lad!' -

He would stamp and scowl and rage: 'I'm not going to bed yet! It's much too early!'

Well, one stormy night the boy's mother couldn't be bothered with him any more.

'I'm going up to bed, myself,' she said. 'But *you* can stay up all night, for all I care!'

She climbed up the ladder to the loft, taking the lamp with her; and as soon as she was settled in her bed, she blew it right out.

'You can see how you like it down there in the dark on your own,' she called. 'Especially when the *fairies* come out to get you!'

'Fairies!' scoffed the boy. 'You can't frighten me, Mam!' And he settled down to spend the night in the kitchen.

It was very dark, so he crept to the stove and opened the door. Under their shroud of ashes, the logs glowed with a dull, red light.

The boy grew bored. He fidgeted. He drummed his feet on the

hearth and gave a loud sigh: *'Hhhh!'*

At this, the logs shifted inside the firebox. Then all at once, a weird, reedy voice called out:

'What's the matter with you, then?'

The boy jumped. That wasn't his mother - he could hear *her* snoring away up in the loft. His skin prickled.

'Who... who's there?' he whispered.

'It's only me,' answered the voice.

It seemed to be coming from deep inside the stove. The boy crept closer and peered in. A dark, spindly shape scuttled over the ashes and slipped down the fender onto the hearthstone. It stood on its two legs, tossed its head and stared at him.

'Scared of me, are you?' it said.

'N... no,' whispered the boy.

He was shaking, but he mustered courage and squatted down to see the thing properly. It was an elf-girl, no bigger than his hand. Her clothes were the colour of sodden peat. Her hair was bleached gold, like dead grass.

The boy put out his hand and touched her. At once she spat at him:

'Oi! Don't you poke me! Who do you think you are? What's your name?'

'I'm not telling,' the boy said quickly.

The elf-girl tutted. 'Don't make me angry,' she hissed, 'or I'll work evil spells on you. Hurry up: tell me who you are!'

The boy thought to himself: *I could play her at her own game.* So aloud he said:

'I'm... I'm Only Me.'

The elf-girl gave a coarse laugh. 'I like that!' she said. 'That's a good one. Tell you what: I'll grant you a wish in return. What do you want?'

'Magic!' answered the boy at once. 'I wish for some magic tricks!'

14

The elf-girl nodded. She scuttled back into the fire and scooped up a handful of ash. She spat on it, kneaded it like dough and shaped it into animals, each the size of a thumbnail: wolf, badger, weasel, rat.

Then she blew on them. The shapes shuddered, glowed and grew warm. They began to move. Claws stretched. Tails waved. Tongues slithered over teeth.

The boy was too astonished to speak.

'Lost your tongue?' the elf-girl snapped at him. 'Well, if you've got nothing to say, make yourself useful instead. I'm tired after all that magic. I feel cold. Go on: stoke up the fire!'

The boy picked up the poker and prodded half-heartedly at the smouldering logs.

The elf-girl hummed with impatience and kicked him. 'Bash it, you weakling!' she cried.

The boy thumped the poker down heavily. *Zoosh!* Flames seared up and a mass of red-hot cinders flew into the air. They scattered down like shooting stars... and landed on the elf-girl's foot.

She let out a heart-numbing, unearthly shriek.

There was a moment of dead silence. Then the wind came moaning down the chimney - and *another* eerie voice called out:

'Who's that? What's the matter?'

'It's only me, Mother,' the elf-girl called back. 'He's burnt my foot, that's what's the matter!'

'Burnt your foot, did he?' hissed the other voice. 'Well, you just tell me who did it, my girl. I'll snare him in my spells! I'll freeze his heart! I'll make him suffer ten times worse than you have!'

Slowly, trembling, the boy inched away from the stove. He slipped behind a large chair in the farthest corner of the room. He was damp with sweat. He held his breath.

'Who did it?' said the elf-girl. 'I can easily tell you that, Mother, because he told me his name. It was... Only Me.'

The hidden one let out a hideous groan. 'You stupid child!' it cried. 'If it was only you that hurt yourself, what's all the fuss about, eh?'

Rain drummed on the roof and the wind howled. Behind the chair, the boy could hardly move with fear. But he forced himself to peer out. And this is what he saw:

Down the chimney came a long, long arm, and at its end was a transparent, bone-pale hand with scratchy fingers clutching at the fire. The flames flickered beneath them.

The fingers found what they were seeking: the elf-girl. They snatched her up by her ears and shook her hard.

Then a thick cloud of soot came pouring down the chimney. The elf-girl screamed. The fire went right out. In the blackness, everything vanished.

That boy scooted up the ladder as fast as he could - and straight into bed beside his poor, long suffering mother. You can be sure he never saw anything like it again.

For every night of his life after that, until he was a bent old man, he always went to bed really early!

THE BABY IN THE RIVER

A man lived in a splendid mansion on the banks of the River Coquet. This man had once been rich, but he was an incurable gambler and he'd lost all his fortune to gaming tables and drink.

One day the gambler received this letter from abroad:

My dear old friend,

You may be surprised to hear from me, as many years have passed since our bitter argument. I hope we can put this behind us now, as I have both good news and bad news to share with you.

Firstly, the good: I have a baby son!

But tragically, my beloved wife died in childbirth. To make matters worse, at almost the same time, I fell seriously ill, and the doctors say I don't have long to live. So our poor, new-born son will very soon be an orphan.

I am therefore arranging for a nurse to bring him to you in Northumberland, so that you and your own wife can care for him and bring him up. I know this is a lot to ask. But we have no living relations and, for old time's sake, I'm sure I can trust you to help me out of this deep trouble.

By the way, there is no need to worry about money,
because as soon as I die the child will inherit my entire
fortune, which is very large. And if - God forbid! - he
should die before he grows up, I have arranged for that same
fortune to pass to you.

Thank you so much for your kindness at this difficult
time.

Your once best friend,

J.

The gambler thought about this letter for a long time; but strange to tell, he said nothing of it to his wife.

Several weeks later, another letter arrived. It announced that a nurse would shortly arrive at the mansion bringing the baby who was now, indeed, an orphan. Still the gambler did not discuss it with his wife. Instead he sent her out on a long errand on the appointed day. He received the baby by himself and sent the nurse away hastily, assuring her that she was not needed.

The baby was sound asleep. The gambler did not even bother to look at him properly. He was too busy sending a message to some gypsies that were camped nearby. The message asked their leader to carry out a small job for him, for which he would be well paid.

The gypsy came to the mansion by return. The gambler handed him the baby, wrapped in swaddling clothes.

'Take this child away to the river,' he said coldly. 'Then drown him!'

'I can't do that, sir,' said the gypsy, horrified. 'That's murder!'

'And this is gold,' said the gambler. He showed the gypsy a large golden coin that he'd won only the night before at the gaming tables. 'It'll be yours if you do what I tell you.'

The gypsy didn't say 'yes' and he didn't say 'no'. He snatched the gold coin and slipped it quickly into his pocket. Then, carrying the baby like a bundle of firewood, he hurried from the room.

On the way out of the servants' door, he bumped into the housekeeper. Quickly he hid the baby behind his back.

'What's that you've got?' she demanded, for she was suspicious of the travelling people.

'Can't tell you nothing, missus,' said he. 'But I'm a God fearing man and I swear this to you: I shan't do no wrong!'

The housekeeper stared after him as he disappeared down the path. She thought she heard a whimper coming from the bundle he was hiding, and wondered if her master had given him some kittens to drown. But why did he seem so shifty about it?

The gypsy was shaking like a leaf by the time he reached the River Coquet. He had a family himself, and nothing would persuade him to do the evil deed. As he stood by the water, wondering what to do, he heard a shout. A fisherman was hurrying towards him.

The gypsy panicked. He knew too well that everyone thought the worst of his people: they always got the blame for any trouble. He laid the baby carefully on the bank, then turned and plunged into the river. He swam straight across and ran like the wind, back to his camp. There he ordered all his kinsfolk to pack up and harness their horses. Within no time they had all disappeared to the other end of the country.

As the gypsy fled, the fisherman reached the river. He saw the baby lying in the grass and gently picked it up. The baby woke and began to cry. The fisherman had no child of his own, not even a wife, but he was a kindly man. When the baby gazed up at him, it sent a flood of warmth through his heart. He decided to take it home and try to look after it himself.

He took the baby back to his cottage and unwrapped the swaddling. A gold locket was hanging round the baby's neck. The fisherman opened it. Inside were two miniature portraits of a wealthy looking woman and man - clearly the child's parents. The fisherman stared at them for a while. Then he hid the locket carefully under his mattress.

He turned out to be a very good foster-father. Several shepherds' wives lived nearby and they gladly helped him with milk and good advice. Soon the baby grew into a strapping boy and then into a strong, quick-witted youth. He eagerly learned everything the fisherman taught him, from catching river fish and digging drains for a living, to reading the Bible and writing poetry. The fisherman was very proud of him.

Meanwhile, the gambler had stolen the child's fortune. Of course, this had been his intention from the outset. However, he quickly lost it all at the gaming tables. But no matter: he soon forgot about it, *and* about his young nephew. For he had a child of his own now, a beautiful daughter.

Just like the orphaned boy, the girl's mother had died in childbirth, so the gambler had had to raise her on his own. Luckily, she had not inherited any of her father's greed or malice. She was sweet natured and generous. Being so different, she couldn't stand her father's company. To escape him, she often went for long walks alone.

One day she was walking along the Coquet when the bank gave way. She slipped and fell in! It was at a place where the water flowed both fast and deep, and she wasn't strong enough to swim against the current. She screamed and thrashed about desperately...

By chance, the fisherman's foster-son happened to be passing by. As soon as he heard her screams, he flung off his jacket, dived in and hauled her to safety.

'Oh, thank you!' the girl cried when she had got her breath back.

'You've saved my life! Who are you and where do you live? I'm sure my father will want to pay you a reward.'

'Oh, I don't want anything like that,' said the youth, smiling into her eyes. 'The only reward I would like is to see you again.'

The girl was very happy to agree. And so they started to meet regularly. First it was week by week; and then day by day. Before long, they had fallen in love.

They were both old enough to get married. The fisherman was very happy to give them his blessing. But the girl's father classed himself as gentry, and when he discovered that her sweetheart was one of the common people, he immediately refused.

'Whatever can we do?' the boy asked his foster father. 'Can you think of anything, anything at all, that might change her father's mind?'

The fisherman racked his brains. Suddenly he remembered the gold locket which had lain hidden under his mattress for all those years. He took it out, opened it and gave it to the boy.

'Show this to your girl's father up at the mansion,' he said. 'You were wearing it when I rescued you from the river bank as a tiny baby. I've always assumed that these must be your real parents. By the look of them, you must have been born into a fine, wealthy family. When her father realises you're not really just an ordinary fellow like me, maybe he'll change his mind.'

The boy took the locket and hurried to the mansion. The old housekeeper welcomed him in, for she knew how the girl loved him. But her master refused to see the boy.

'Even if he won't see me,' begged the boy, 'please ask him to look at this.'

He opened the locket and gave it to the housekeeper. She glanced down at the pictures - and at once the blood drained from her face.

'Oh!' she exclaimed. 'These pictures are the very image of my master's old friend and his wife! I used to see them a lot in the days before they quarrelled with my master. Then they moved abroad - and sadly both of them are long dead. Where on earth did you get this?'

The boy told her. 'I didn't know about this locket until today,' he added. 'My foster father had always told me I was left on the river bank by a gypsy.'

'A gypsy!'cried the housekeeper. Her mind flashed back through the years to that strange afternoon when a gypsy had rushed past her, trying to hide a bundle that seemed to be alive. Suddenly everything fell into place. 'Then you must be the son of my master's friend!' she cried. 'When he died abroad, my master inherited his fortune. It was said there were no blood heirs. *You* were really his heir, but my master thought he had killed you. By rights, the fortune should have been yours. Oh, I never thought he could be so wicked!'

The boy did not wait to hear any more. He rushed into the gambler's sitting room, showed him the locket and told him everything. The gambler could not possibly argue against such proof.

'Give me back the money you stole from me, you rogue!' shouted the boy. He pulled his fish-knife from his belt. 'Or else, come outside and fight a duel!'

'I can't give it back to you,' replied the gambler, trembling. 'I've already spent or lost the lot.'

'Then give me your mansion instead,' said the boy. He came closer and drew himself up to his full height. 'And let me marry your daughter.'

The gambler nodded quickly. 'Yes, yes,' he stuttered, 'take her - take the house - take everything I have. Only please, my boy, spare my life. After all, your father was once my good friend...'

'And this is how you rewarded his friendship!'retorted the boy. 'Why should I spare you after you tried to *murder* me?'

'I'll get out of your way at once,' gabbled the gambler. 'I'll leave Northumberland - I swear I'll never come back!'

He rushed out, saddled his horse and galloped away. After that he was never heard of again.

When his daughter came into the room, she was astonished to hear what had happened. She was also overjoyed. For she had always hated her evil father. And she was thrilled to discover that nothing could now keep her from the boy she loved.

They got married without delay and took over the mansion. The boy's foster-father moved in with them, and was able to retire. The housekeeper retired too, but they begged her to stay living there, since it was thanks to her that the true story had been revealed.

Maybe you're thinking that romance might brew between the old fisherman and the old housekeeper? Well, it's not for me to deny it! But there's one thing I can tell you with great certainty: all four of them lived happily by the banks of the River Coquet until the end of their days.

THE NIGHT DWARFS

'Where the hell have you been?' she said. 'I've been waiting up for you all night!'

'I took a short cut over the hills,' he said.

'That's the longest short cut *I've* ever heard of,' she said. 'Even walking slowly, it's only 15 minutes by road from Rothbury to here. I suppose you got lost, you old fool?'

'The mist came down,' he said. 'And what with it being dark, I could only see two yards ahead. I almost had a heart attack when they jumped out at me!'

'Jumped out?' she said. 'What on earth are you talking about?'

'Dwarfs they were,' he said.

'Dwarfs!' she said. 'Well, I don't need to ask if you've been drinking!'

'Me?' he said. 'Never! Eh, but I've never seen such ugly little creatures. No more than knee high, they were, and their beards curling up to their noses!'

'Just a minute!' she said. 'How come you could see them so clearly? You've just told me it was completely misty and dark.'

'Ah,' he said, 'they were carrying torches, see? You know, the old fashioned sort like in pictures, with flames burning at the end. And in the other hand, they were all holding clubs.'

'Clubs!' she said. 'You'll be telling me next that they beat you up!'

'Well,' he said, 'they did chase after me... but I grabbed a stick off the ground and managed to give some of them a good thrashing. *That* sent them scattering! I thought I'd got rid of them for good. And that's when I saw the light.'

'What light's this?' she said.

'Well,' he said, 'it wasn't moving, and it looked kind of welcoming. I reckoned it was shining from a cottage.'

'A *cottage!*' she said. 'Since when have there been any cottages on that part of the Simonside Hills?'

'I couldn't think straight, could I?' he said.

'Not with ten pints or more in you!' she said.

'If I was really so drunk,' he said, 'how come I managed to walk directly to the light without stumbling, eh? Mind you, you're right, when I reached it, I found it wasn't really a cottage after all. It was a shepherd's hut. The door was unlocked. Although no-one was there, I found a nice fire burning in the grate.'

'Why,' she said, 'would anyone light a fire in a shepherd's hut six months after all the lambing's ended?'

'I didn't stop to ask,' he said, 'seeing as I was near frozen with cold. Besides, I was desperate to shut myself away from the little brutes tormenting me outside. So I closed the door tightly behind me and went straight across to the fire.'

'And then?' she said.

'There were two big stones set up like seats,' he said, 'one on each side of the hearth. Eh, it was nice and warm there - I was glad to sit down. That is, until *he* came in.'

'*He?*' she said. 'What, another of your dwarfs?'

'Too right,' he said. 'But this one, he didn't threaten me like the others. In fact, he totally ignored me. Just sat down on the other side of the fire, didn't say a word.'

'So how long did you stay there?' she said.

'Oh, for the rest of the night,' he said. 'I wasn't going to risk

25

stirring him up by moving about, was I? And I certainly didn't dare go to sleep in case he got up to any tricks. So I just sat there for hours, throwing more logs on the fire and watching the flames. At last it started to get light outside. And then it vanished.'

'Vanished?' she said. 'What, the dwarf?'

'Yes, him,' he said, 'and also the hut. Everything! Even the fire had burnt itself out. There was nothing left of it except ashes.'

'Oh, you poor idiot,' she said. 'And I suppose you were shivering with cold?'

'I was,' he said, 'and shivering with fright, too. Because now I could see that the stone where I was sitting was right on the edge of a rocky crag! Look out the window, you can see it from here - that one just below the skyline with a sheer drop beneath it. Lucky I hadn't dozed off!'

'Just up *there?*' she said. 'But that would have taken you no time to get home! You don't really expect me to believe all this moonshine, do you?'

'Why ever not?' he said.

THE SORCERER, THE KNIGHT AND THE WITCH

A thick sea-mist once came rolling in over the sheep pastures; and when it cleared, there was a sorcerer on the road!

I don't know where he came from, but he was a sour-faced brute of a fellow, mounted on a demon-horse that snorted fire from its nostrils like a dragon. He rode at a leisurely pace, staring around from sunken, bloodshot eyes. By the time he reached the village it was nightfall.

The villagers screamed when they saw him: they all rushed inside their cottages and bolted their doors. The sorcerer cursed at their backs. Then he went down to the river, built a fire, hung a cauldron over it and crammed it full of weird ingredients. Soon it was bubbling away, giving off a foul smelling steam.

Next morning, the villagers peered out, hoping and praying the sorcerer would be gone. Unfortunately he wasn't. And his spells had conjured up something extraordinary: a huge, ugly castle!

This castle was built like a fortress with towering battlements and heavy iron doors. It stood right in the middle of the river, on a mound made of devilish black, sticky mud. It dammed the river so that the water couldn't flow past it. It turned all the water black too and made it spill over onto the fields.

'*Now* what'll we do?' grumbled the village women. 'We can't use this filthy water to drink or for washing!'

'Can't let the sheep drink from it either,' said their husbands.

A group of them went to complain to the sorcerer. Realising he was a dangerous man, they were careful to be very polite.

'Would you be good enough, sir,' they said, 'to work another spell, to make the river clean again?'

But the sorcerer didn't go in for goodness.

'This is how I like water to be,' he said, 'black and thick, to feed my soul with the Devil's darkness. It's *my* river now, for I've built my castle over it. The best thing you simpletons can do is get out of here before it poisons you!' And he laughed so loudly that they could see right down his throat into the gaping hole of his gullet.

The villagers couldn't believe this disaster. After a hurried meeting, they packed their few humble belongings into chests and bags, loaded them onto carts and fled into the hills. What else could they do? For the sorcerer was clearly in league with the Devil. If they didn't get away from him fast, there was no knowing what evil things might happen!

They hadn't travelled very far before they saw someone coming along the road towards them. It was a knight. He was dressed in full armour and riding a fine grey horse. As they drew closer, the knight leaped to the ground and bowed.

'Hail, good people!' he said. 'Where are you all off to in such a hurry? - and why?'

'We're off to make a new start in the hill country,' said one of the women; and she told him all about the sorcerer.

'Oh dear!' cried the knight, 'not that evil villain! I've had dealings with him myself. We had a quarrel once, that turned into a sword fight. Just as I had almost beat him, the rogue threw down his sword like a coward and started using magic instead. He worked the most terrible, tricksy spells to cut off both my hands and feet.'

The villagers stared at him in puzzlement.

'But you look all right to me,' said another woman.

'Yes indeed,' said the knight, 'I'm fully recovered now. I was cured at an amazing place that lies not far from here. I'll tell you how to find it, because it might help you too. Keep going to the end of this road, through the wolf forest and into the hills. Where the road ends, you'll see a crooked cottage, and next to it there's a fine, bubbling spring. This spring flows into a rushing burn, and from there into the river. The water of this spring is amazingly sweet, and it also has miraculous healing powers. When I drank from the spring and bathed in the burn, my hands and feet grew back again as if the sorcerer had never chopped them off! I swear it's true.'

'But what about the crooked cottage that stands beside it?' said one of the men. 'Does anyone live there?'

'I was just coming to that,' said the knight. 'This crooked house is the home of a witch, and the bubbling spring and its burn actually belong to her. She's an ill tempered old hag and she doesn't normally let anyone share her magic water. *But...* she and the sorcerer are great enemies. Once she hears the trouble he's caused, she's sure to help you.'

The villagers thanked the knight and continued on their journey. They followed the road straight through the forest. The sun set and it grew dark: clouds of bats came out and close by a pack of wolves howled. But they went boldly on, holding twinkling lanterns to light their way. When they emerged from the far side of the forest, the moon came up. By its light they climbed up a steep path that dipped up and down through knee-high swathes of heather. It stopped abruptly in a hollow where they could hear a spring bubbling noisily. Just beside the spring stood a crooked old cottage.

One of the men went up and knocked on the door. It was opened by the witch herself! She was a bent old crone with warts on her long nose and cobwebs in her hair.

'What do you want?' she hissed. 'Get out of here, or I'll turn you all into maggots with my spells!'

'Don't do that, good lady,' begged the man. Quickly he told her everything that had happened.

'So!' said the witch, 'that sorcerer is *your* enemy too, is he? In that case, you must be my friends, and you are more than welcome. Just wait here.'

She went back into her cottage. As the dawn broke they heard weird sounds coming from inside, and acrid smoke rose from her chimney. Suddenly one of the children gave a shout:

'Eh! Look behind!'

When they turned round they saw a whole new village standing on the slope above the spring!

They made a good life up there in the hills. Though it was a deal colder, the bubbling spring waters kept them and their sheep nice and healthy. So things were fine for a while.

But nothing stays perfect for long, does it? The change came because the sorcerer owned a marvellous magic ring. This ring wasn't made of metal but of stone, and when he looked through it, he could see things happening a long way off. That's how he found out that the villagers were living happily up at the bubbling spring.

'Spitting serpents!' he cried. 'I wanted those villagers to starve and die! I can guess exactly how they've escaped me: it's due to that interfering old witch! Ach! I shall have to go up to the bubbling spring and root her out!'

The sorcerer buckled his iron sword to his belt and jumped onto his fiery demon-horse. He rode at a gallop along the road up through the wolf forest, to the hill of the bubbling spring. The sheep saw him coming and ran away in terror. The children fled indoors, wailing. But the sorcerer wasn't interested in them. No, it was the witch he was after!

The witch came straight out and poked her warty face at him with a hoot of laughter. The sorcerer snapped his fingers, sending out a lightning bolt so that her raggedy hair burst into flames. She shook them out - and hit back at him with a handful of filthy spell-dust that made him shudder and jump and squeal.

The sorcerer soon realised that her magic was a match for his. So he turned instead to ordinary brute force. He seized his sword, rushed at the witch and drove its blade through her heart. The witch shrieked - and dropped dead.

The sorcerer stood gloating over her body. Then he leaped back onto his demon-horse with a roar of triumph. But just then, who should appear but the knight!

The sorcerer cackled at the sight of him and waved his staff, thinking he could destroy the knight with a few simple spells. But he had reckoned without the knight's horse, which was a plucky stallion. Seeing its master in mortal danger, it charged at the sorcerer's demon-horse, kicking with its hooves and biting with its long, sharp teeth.

The demon-horse tried to snort fire in return, but fear made the flames freeze up its nostrils. It gave a bray of terror, turned and bolted, with the sorcerer clinging to it, all the way back to the castle.

'You can come out, good people!' the knight shouted. 'The villain's gone!'

The villagers were delighted to see their old friend and gathered eagerly around him.

'Just watch this,' the knight said. He heaved the body of the dead witch into the middle of the bubbling spring.

The villagers were sorry to see the witch was dead: although she was a nasty hag, she had helped them a lot. Also they were horrified to see the knight polluting the spring. But the knight winked at them.

'All in a good cause,' he grinned 'Watch her last trick!'

The waters of the bubbling spring began to froth. They rose up around the witch's body until they had turned into a great, foaming flood. The flood spilt over and poured down the hill, carrying the witch's body with it.

The knight led the villagers to the the top of the hill to get a good view. They saw the flood pouring into the meadow like a burn swollen with winter snow-melt. Soon it reached their old village, where the sorcerer's castle now stood. It swirled right through the castle. When it came gushing out on the other side, it was carrying two more bodies beside the witch. One was the demon-horse, and the other was the sorcerer.

The flood raced on and on until it reached the sand dunes. There it forced its way through a gully, across the beach and down to the open sea, taking the witch, the sorcerer and his demon-horse with it. No-one ever found their bodies. So they must still be lost down there, in the salty bottom of the ocean.

After that, the knight and the villagers all went home again. The knight moved into the witch's old house and became the new guardian of the bubbling spring. He made a much better job of it than the witch had done, and gave a fine welcome to anyone who wanted to taste its waters.

That's how things stayed for many years, until the children up there had all grown up and moved away for work and weddings, and the knight and the older villagers had all died.

All this happened so long ago that you won't find any trace of their cottages up there now. Of course, the bubbling spring is still there, because waters like that never stop flowing - but I'm not going to tell you where to find it!

THE WEDDING GHOSTS

Every year, but once a year,
the ghosts go riding by:
a moon-pale bride, her groom and men.
Each turns a fearsome eye
upon her lover, stained with blood,
who caused them all to die!

There was a man and a girl who fell in love.

The man - Ridley they called him - was a strong, handsome
fellow, oozing charm; but he came from a rough family - the kind
that was always fighting - and he was short of money. He knew all
along that there was no chance of marrying the lovely Abigail. For
her father was the rich and powerful Baron of Featherstone, and he
wanted a husband of the same class for his daughter. To make
matters even worse, their two families were long-standing enemies.

For months Ridley and Abigail met in secret, hiding in the woods
that surrounded the Baron's castle. Then one day, she brought him
the news they had both been dreading.

'My father says I have to get married to someone else,' she told
him. 'He's fixed the wedding for next week.'

Ridley's grip on her tightened: 'Who's he giving you to?'

'A rich landowner from the south,' said Abigail. She started
weeping. 'He's fat and bad tempered - I can't stand him!'

'Refuse him,' said Ridley.

'I can't,' said Abigail. 'My father has a will of iron. He'll beat me until I say "yes".'

Ridley thought fast. 'Then run away with me,' he said. 'Now!'

'I would,' said Abigail, 'honestly I would... only... is it true what I've heard, that you have no money? How will you keep me?'

'I'll keep you in love,' said Ridley. 'Isn't that enough for you?

'Almost,' she said. 'Only... what will we live on?'

'We'll live on our wits together,' he said breathlessly, 'like I've done on my own until now.'

But Abigail shook her head and pushed him gently away. 'Maybe you're not the one for me after all,' she said. 'I can't give up my jewels and my featherbed, no matter how much I love you.'

Then she turned and ran back to her father's castle.

Ridley was like the rest of his clan: he couldn't bear to be slighted. When Abigail rejected him, he felt wounded in his heart. It grew more painful day by day. And the pain twisted him: it turned his love for her into hate.

He brooded and complained to his friends and kinsmen about the jilting. Every time he spoke of it, the story grew bigger and more bitter. Soon he'd gathered round him a whole band of sympathetic men. They slandered the girl for leading him on, and then dropping him to marry money. One phrase was on every man's lips:

'You've got to take revenge!'

On the day of Abigail's wedding, Ridley led his band into the woods outside Featherstone Castle. Each one was armed with a sword.

They waited there patiently all day. They waited while Abigail and her groom went to Haltwhistle Church to get married. They waited while the wedding party came back to the castle for their feast.

Night fell. The moon came up. The time drew near.

There was an old tradition in the Baron's family: every time there was a wedding, the feast would end with the bride and groom and the groom's men riding right round the bounds of the castle lands. Everyone in the area knew about this custom - that's why Ridley and his band were waiting in the woods.

They heard the distant sound of hoofs and the jingle of harnesses as the wedding party came out. The riders skirted the low fields.

An owl soared through the air, shrieking. The riders turned up towards the woods.

'Now!' growled Ridley - and his band pounced.

They hauled the groom and his men from their horses, wrestled them to the ground and lashed at them with their swords. Abigail screamed. She looked lovelier than ever in her flowing white wedding gown, but Ridley was blinded to her beauty. He cheered as his men's blades tore into her men's flesh; but he kept the groom for himself, finishing him off in an orgy of metal and blood.

Then he turned to Abigail.

The girl was weeping and swooning with misery and terror. With a crazed laugh, Ridley wrenched her from the saddle and clasped her in his arms. He wiped his blood-stained sword on his trousers, then held it to her throat.

'If I can't have you, *my love,*' he hissed, 'then no-one shall!'

And he killed her.

So all was done. The men in his band nodded at Ridley and drifted away. Now only Ridley himself was left there under the cold moonlight, with seven dead men at his feet, and beside them the body of Abigail.

He fell to his knees and gazed at her. One last time, he ran his hand down her cheek and put his lips to hers. How cold they felt, how cold!

The smouldering pain in his heart flared up like a fire in the wind. He groaned and tightened his fingers on his sword. He turned the blade - threw himself onto it - and dropped, slowly, to the ground beside his former sweetheart.

The moon inched across the sky. Clouds scudded past it. The dead bodies lay still. Hours dripped by.

One by one, silently, the bodies rose.

They were paler than the moon: transparent, like gossamer or water. Ghosts, they'd become already - grieving spirits of the troubled dead.

Their horses had long since bolted. But the ghosts whistled - and phantom horses came. The ghosts mounted them in the dark, one to each horse. Only Ridley and Abigail shared a saddle.

Stiff faced, in single file, slow and solemn, they rode towards the Baron's castle. They passed as vapour through fence, wall, tree and the castle doors.

The wedding guests screamed at the sight of them and the minstrels stopped their music; but the ghosts made no sign or sound. They moved around the hall. They passed the high table, leaving food untouched yet tainted. Still without a word they passed back through the doors and melted into the night.

All the guests fled. Later, the servants found the Baron on the floor, collapsed from fear, horror and heartbreak.

He recovered for a while; but on the anniversary of the wedding he saw the ghostly procession again, and that was the end of him. He was struck dumb and paralysed, and soon after that he died.

But the memory of that terrible night lives on to haunt his castle. For still:

Every year, but once a year,
the ghosts go riding by:
a moon-pale bride, her groom and men.
Each turns a fearsome eye
upon her lover, stained with blood,
who caused them all to die!

THE MAGIC OINTMENT

A farm worker and his wife were the only couple in Netherwitton
who had no children. They longed for a baby with all their hearts,
but years went by and their wish was never granted. And so they
grew sadder and sadder.

'If I can't have a child of my own,' the wife said at last, 'I'd just
as soon adopt one. If only some poor, needy little bairn would come
our way!'

One dark winter's night soon after that, there came an urgent
knocking at their cottage door. The farm worker hurried to open it.
Outside a terrible blizzard was blowing up and it was freezing. A
very strange looking couple were standing on the doorstep. The
woman was cradling a tiny, sleeping baby in her arms.

'Good grief!' cried the farm worker at once, 'You'd better come
in and get warm!' For the strangers were not at all prepared for the
weather: their clothes were more suitable for a ball than a storm.
They were beautifully cut but fine-spun and flimsy, and there was a
fair bit of gold jewellery glimmering from under their flowing
cloaks.

The strange woman smiled at the farm worker and shook her head.
'No, no,' she said in a fluting voice, 'don't bother about us: we're
fine. It's the little one we're worried about. We're wondering if you
and your wife could take care of him for a while? We'd pay you
well.'

'Of course,' the farm worker said at once. 'But where are you going? When will you be back to collect him?'

The strange woman didn't answer. Instead she pulled out a fat leather purse and pressed it into his hand. Then she gave him the baby.

The strangers turned to go. But at the last minute, the man whispered something urgently into the woman's ear and she turned back to the farm worker with a cry.

'Oh!' she said, 'I almost forgot to give you this. Take great care of it now, and don't forget to use it every day.'

'What is it?' asked the farm worker.

'Ointment,' said the strange woman. 'You must rub some into the little one's eyes every morning and night, without fail.'

'Yes of course,' said the farm worker, 'but...'

The strange man looked at him severely. 'Make sure you always wash your hands after using it,' he said. 'And whatever you do, *don't let any get into your own eyes,* because it's dangerous.'

'Then how...?' began the farm worker. But the strange couple had already reached the end of the path and were passing through the gate. They disappeared into the whirling snowflakes and the night.

When the farm worker went back inside carrying a baby in his arms, his wife was astonished.

'Wherever did you get that baby from?' she cried

'The people at the door.'

'But who were they?'

'I don't know.'

'When are they coming back for it?'

'They didn't say,' said the farm worker. 'They just asked me to look after it for a while. And... they paid me with this.'

He showed his wife the purse. She took the baby from him while he emptied it onto the table. They both shrieked with wonder when they saw what it contained.

'That's gold, that is - real gold!'

'We're rich!'

But though the wife was thrilled with the gold, even better was holding a real live baby in her arms. She rocked it up and down and cooed at it. The baby smiled at her with big, dark eyes. He was a pretty, elfin looking little thing. She was so happy nursing him, she soon forgot all her questions. The farm worker was delighted too. He got out his tool-kit and, with a bit of clever hammering and sawing, soon turned a drawer into a fine cradle for the child. As they sang him to sleep that night, they were the happiest people in the whole village.

The next morning they woke with great joy to the baby's gurgling. They spent all day feeding and playing with him. As the hours went by, they began to dread his real parents coming back to fetch him; but they didn't.

It was the same the next day, and the day after that. Then the days turned to weeks, the weeks into months and the months into years. In all that time, the strange man and woman never came back.

No matter, the farm worker and his wife were ecstatically happy with the child, and he was happy with them. He grew up to be slim, nimble and quick witted. Also, he had an extraordinary talent for music. As soon as he was old enough, he learned to play the fiddle, and though he couldn't read music, he played tunes so beautiful that it made people cry.

That was one unusual thing about him. The other was the problem with his eyes. Ever since they'd had the boy, the farm worker and his wife had taken care to rub ointment into his eyes twice a day, just as the strangers had ordered. If they were ever late about it, the boy used to whine: 'Hurry up and do my eyes, I can't see things properly without the ointment.'

'Do you think we should take him to the doctor about this?' the wife wondered.

'No, no, his eyes and his sight are both quite normal, so long as he has the ointment applied,' the farm worker answered.

'But what'll we do once the pot runs out? - as it's bound to soon,' she said.

'But *will* it?' said the farm worker. 'We've been using it for nearly seven years now, yet there still seems plenty of it left! It doesn't look as if it'll *ever* run out to me.'

Well, this conversation stayed in the farm worker's mind and haunted him. He couldn't stop thinking about that ointment, wondering what it was made of, what it did and exactly how it worked.

One night his wife went out to visit her mother, leaving him in charge of putting the boy to bed. The farm worker tucked him up as usual, then applied the ointment to the boy's eyes and said goodnight. But this time he didn't wash the curious stuff off his hands straight away. Instead he tipped his fingers back into the pot - and rubbed some of it into one of his own eyes.

Nothing happened.

It didn't sting or tingle. It didn't affect his vision. It didn't do *anything*.

So the farm worker forgot about it, and things carried on as usual.

A few months later, a big fair came to Longhorsely, a village nearby. The boy begged the farm worker and his wife to take him to it, so they did. It was a marvellous event, crammed with many exciting stalls, and very crowded.

The farm worker went off to watch the wrestling, leaving his wife to look after the boy. A high old time she had with him! For he kept running off. And every time she caught up with him, he was behaving very oddly. He seemed to be talking to the empty air - and the words he used were all nonsense. The wife scolded him and slapped him, but he wouldn't stop. She didn't know what to do, so she went and fetched her husband.

'There he is!' she cried, pointing at the boy in the distance. They crept closer. 'Just listen to that gibberish he's talking! There's not even anyone there to hear it.'

'Of course there is,' said the farm worker. 'Can't you see that little man he's talking to? Not that I like the look of him.'

'What man?' said his wife.

'The one in the brown coat and the green breeches, with the long fair hair.'

'I can't see anyone,' said the wife crossly. 'You need your head examined, you do: you're turning as odd as the boy!'

The farm worker felt insulted at these words, but also a bit uncomfortable. So while his wife grabbed the boy and scolded him for wandering off yet again, the farm worker went slouching off on his own to brood. There was something disturbing about the little man that the boy had been talking to, but he couldn't work out what it was. And why couldn't his wife see him?

As he trudged around the fairground, the farm worker began to notice that there were quite a few other strange people hanging about, women as well as men. They all had similar colouring to the little man - pale and washed out - with slender limbs, quick, ethereal movements and old fashioned, flowing clothes.

Quite a few of them seemed to be pickpockets and thieves - and they were quite open about it. He saw several of them putting out their hands and snatching trinkets or baskets of cheese from the stalls, right in front of the stall-holders' eyes.

But the stall-holders didn't seem to care. They didn't even seem to notice.

Maybe it's only us that can see them, the farm worker thought to himself, *just me and the boy.*

But why should that be?

Suddenly it came to him: the ointment!

He decided to do an experiment. He remembered that he'd only rubbed the ointment into one eye. So next time he saw some of the strange people, he covered up the ointment eye.

Sure enough, when he looked at them with just the other eye, they all seemed to turn invisible.

He began to feel afraid. He guessed that the ointment was magic. He realised that, having used it once, he'd never be able to get rid of it.

He ambled nervously through the crowd. And suddenly who should he see but the strange couple who had brought the boy to their cottage, all of seven years ago!

He pushed his way through to them and tapped the strange woman on the shoulder. As she turned to him, he caught the familiar glimmer of gold on her fingers and sparkling at her throat. She gasped when she saw it was him.

'Hello there, my friends,' said the farm worker. 'Well, it's good to meet you again! I'm pleased to say that the child you left with us is doing very well. He's grown into quite a big lad now and...'

The strange woman said nothing. But the strange man grabbed the farm worker by the shirt and growled:

'You fool! You stole some of that magic ointment for yourself, didn't you! Which eye do you see us with?'

'No... I... but...' the farm worker stammered.

'Which eye?' the stranger roared at him. He threw back his hood angrily. The farm worker saw gold glimmering amongst his thick, flaxen curls.

'Th... this one, sir,' the farm worker said nervously, pointing to the eye where he'd applied the ointment.

The strange man leaned towards him. He blew on the magicky eye. At once he and the woman and the other strange people haunting the fairground all vanished!

From that moment, the farm worker was completely blind in the eye where he had rubbed the magic ointment.

Also, the little boy that he and his wife had fostered for seven wonderful years disappeared at the fairground. Although they and their neighbours searched high and low for him, he was never seen again.

The farm worker and his wife were heartbroken. But they still had most of the gold left, and every time they spent some, it reminded them of their foster son and brought them some comfort. Besides, they realised now they were lucky to have kept the child for as long as they did....

For they had solved the mystery of where the child had come from, and who his parents were. It was obvious, when they put the pieces of the puzzle together: they were the king and queen of the fairies!

THE SLEEPING KING

There was a young shepherd who kept his flock on the hills near Hadrian's Wall. One summer's day this shepherd caught his ankle in a rabbit hole. As he stumbled to keep his balance, his lunch pack of bread and cheese tipped out of his pocket into an overgrown tangle of nettles, thistles and bracken. He cursed and dived down after it, but no matter how hard he looked he couldn't find it. The shepherd's stomach was rumbling with hunger. He threw himself desperately onto his hands and knees, and pushed his way through the prickles and stinging stems. The sun was hot and the insects droned. He began to feel light headed.

When he straightened up, the bracken stems had grown impossibly tall, meeting far above him in an eerie green tunnel. The wind rustled down it; and he thought he heard a voice calling, *'This way! Hurry this way!'* He spun round and glimpsed a strange figure beckoning to him in the distance: an old man with a long, white beard and a flowing robe. An adder slid past his feet. The walls of the tunnel quivered... and slowly fused into solid stone.

The shepherd felt dizzy and confused, but he stumbled on down it. The tunnel widened and opened into an enormous cave.

No, not a cave but a *hall*. The kind of hall you might find in a medieval castle, with logs blazing in a huge, arched fireplace and dozens of lamps shimmering in black iron chandeliers.

In the centre of the hall stood a vast, round table piled high with delicious food. Around it sat many splendidly dressed knights and ladies, with lithe limbed hunting dogs lying at their feet. But the people and dogs were all slumped against each other or across the table, totally quiet, totally still. Each was lost in a deep, deep sleep.

The shepherd crept in. Slowly, he walked down the hall.

Nobody stirred. Nothing moved. Silence throbbed through the stale air.

The shepherd walked slowly round the table. He came to two golden thrones. On one sat a beautiful, red haired queen, her moon-white hands folded neatly in her lap. Beside her sat a bearded, wise faced king who looked strong enough to wrestle with giants.

The king and the queen were also asleep.

By the king's right hand stood another, smaller table. On it lay two things: a sword in an exquisitely engraved scabbard and a finely polished hunting horn. Carved into the top of the table were the following words:

WELCOME FRIEND!
DO YOU LONG TO BREAK THIS SPELL?
THEN CHOOSE FROM THIS TABLE WELL!
FOR ONLY ONE TREASURE CAN WAKE ARTHUR -
THE ONCE AND FUTURE KING!

The shepherd gave a gasp. Could this *really* be the legendary King Arthur and his wife Queen Guinevere?

He gazed long and carefully at the two objects lying on the table. Which one should he choose? And what should he do with it?

At first he thought it was obvious. Blowing a hunting horn was bound to wake the whole court! Excitedly he picked up the horn and put it to his lips...

But at the last moment, he changed his mind. Surely this was a trick - and blowing a horn was *too* obvious.

So he put down the horn and picked up the sword. It was so heavy, he could scarcely hold it. The hilt was crusted with rubies and emeralds. He grasped it and slowly, slowly pulled it from the scabbard...

Almost at once the hall was filled with sound and movement! King Arthur, Queen Guinevere and the other sleepers sighed, stirred and opened their eyes!

The shepherd was elated. Quicker now, he pulled the sword out further...

There came a great crash of thunder. The chandeliers swung violently and all the candles went out. Now the only light came from the log fire - which had sunk to red, dying embers.

A voice - the same he had heard before - came echoing down the tunnel. *'Oh, vain fool!'* it cried. *'How dare you touch the king's own sword! Why did you not blow the horn to wake him?'*

Before the shepherd could answer, invisible hands seized him. They hurled him across the hall, stumbling over sleeping dogs, knights' outstretched boots and ladies' silken slippers, through the long darkness.... tumbling over and over... then upwards...

Until at last he came to, back on the hill behind the Roman Wall, with his foot awkwardly twisted in a rabbit hole.

The shepherd's heart ached with longing as he limped home. If only he could have a second chance!

Every day after that, for the rest of his life, his thoughts were haunted by the enchanted hall. He yearned to go back there. He searched for hours and miles, scouring every inch of the hills for the strange green tunnel that had led to it.

Poor fool. Of course, he never found it.

SOURCES AND NOTES

For full publication details of all books cited, please see the list at the end, p.55

DRAGON CASTLE

Grice: *Folk Tales of the North Country*
Henderson: *Notes on the Folk Lore of the Northern Counties*
Service: *Metrical Legends of Northumberland*
Leighton: *Wilson's Tales of the Borders*
www.england-in-particular

This is Northumberland's best known and most dramatic folk tale, recorded in many different books. All the sources agree that the castle where the action takes place is at Bamburgh, on the north Northumberland coast.

Most versions are based on an ancient ballad, supposedly composed by Duncan Frasier of Cheviot around 1270. However, www.england-in-particular says that it was most likely composed by the Rev. Robert Norham in the 18th century, perhaps based on authentic local traditions. In this the bewitched princess is called Margaret. The knight is called Childe Wynde and is her brother.

Wilson's Tales of the Borders offers a more intriguing and romantic version in the great Victorian tradition. It claims that the story has its origins in Anglo-Saxon times, and that Bamburgh Castle was originally built by a mighty ancient king. It provides the princess with an Anglo-Saxon name, Agitha, gives equivalent names to all the other characters (anonymous in other sources); says that Childe Wynde was not the princess's brother, but her first cousin (as such, he was a potential marriage partner); and attributes the princess's transformation into a dragon to the intervention of an enchantress. My own retelling is a blend of all these with some extra spice thrown in!

Childe is an archaic name for a youth of noble birth, so I have changed it to 'Young Knight of the Wind' to be less ambiguous. For the other characters, I have stuck to the usual folk tale style of not naming them at all.

Service says a stone at the foot of Bamburgh Castle was supposedly a bewitched maiden, who always wounded anyone who fell against it; Childe Wynde was the only person able to withstand its enchantments.

The story is commonly known by its old name: *'The Laidley Worm of Spindlestone Haugh'*. In old Northumberland dialect *laidley* is 'loathsome'. 'Worm' means a dragon or serpent, from the Old Norse *ormr*. Spindlestone is a small settlement to the west of Bamburgh: in some versions this is where the dragon has its lair. *Haugh* is flood or meadow land in a river valley.

This story contains many typical fairy tale motifs - a wicked stepmother, bewitching of the innocent heroine into a different shape and being rescued by a hero whom she then marries. However, in one aspect it is strikingly different: a dragon is usually an evil beast who devours the princess, rather than being a transformation of her.

ONLY ME

Balfour: *County Folklore - Northumberland*
Briggs: *A Dictionary of British Folk-Tales*
Keightley: *The Fairy Mythology*

Balfour and Keightley say that the story comes from Rothley, a very rural settlement south of Rothbury and just north of Scots Gap, west of Morpeth. Another anecdote in Balfour says that the old mill at Rothley was inhabited by a whole tribe of fairies, who could sometimes be seen bathing by moonlight in the Hart Burn river. They used the mill as their meeting hall and stole grain from the miller as their 'right' for guarding and cleaning the mill. When the miller tried to frighten them away by throwing clods of earth into their fire, they took revenge by bewitching him to be lame.

Briggs found the story in Joseph Jacobs' book, *More English Fairy Tales* and says that the story originally came as a true account from a widow and her son who lived in the village of North Sunderland, near the coast by Seahouses.

THE BABY IN THE RIVER

Briggs: *A Dictionary of British Folk-Tales*

Although Briggs sources this story to the School of Scottish Studies and says it was collected in Selkirkshire (in the Scottish Borders), it is clearly originally from Northumberland. Its original title and subtitle is: *The Drainer of Coquetdale - the Tale of the Coquet*. The

Coquet is one of Northumberland's most spectacular rivers. It rises in the Cheviot Hills west of Alwinton and flows out to the sea at Amble.

The motif of a child left to die but saved by a stranger who raises it to perform heroic deeds and achieve justice is a very common one in world folk tales and myths. One of the oldest and most familiar versions is the Biblical tale of Moses in the bulrushes.

THE NIGHT DWARFS

Grice: *Folk Tales of the North Country*
Ghosts and Legends of Northumbria

This tale is compiled from two linked anecdotes. They are both set in the Simonside Hills which overlook Rothbury. The second source says that shepherds of old claimed these hills to be haunted after dark by ugly, mischievous dwarfs who often ensnared travellers by leading them the wrong way, or into bogs.

Grice calls the dwarfs 'Duergar'. According to Thomas Keightley in *The Fairy Mythology,* these originate in Gothic-German and Norse mythology. They are tiny creatures living in rocks and hills and are skilled in working gold, silver, iron and other metals.

The motif of a house or other refuge offering shelter at night but vanishing by the morning is used in folk tales all over the world and is a common device of tricksters.

THE SORCERER, THE KNIGHT
AND THE WITCH

Tongue: *Forgotten Folk-Tales of the English Counties*

Tongue says that this little-known tale - which she called *Bubbling Well and Black Tarn* - was collected from a Northumberland nurse who was working at a London hospital in the 1920s, and that it may have originated from an old ballad or a medieval romance. The plot is rather muddled, as if it were only half remembered, so I've made sense of it as best I could, and have stayed true to the rapid, chatty narrative style of the original.

No specific location is given for the story: the source simply says that it opens 'near the coast' in a sheltered valley with a stream that 'ran right through it and then fell over the cliffs down to the shore'.

THE WEDDING GHOSTS

Tegner: *Ghosts of the North Country*
Tynedale: *County Legend and Folk-Lore*
Ghosts and Legends of Northumbria

The setting for this is Featherstone Castle which is about three miles from Haltwhistle on the east bank of the South Tyne river, in south-west Northumberland. The baron took his name from the castle, and the surrounding land is known as Featherstonehaugh. Tegner sources the story to *The Monthly Chronicle* of 1888, which gives a full account, and also to *Richardson's Local Historian's Table Book,* undated.

Tynedale says the jilted lover was called Ridley of Hardriding and that their two families had a long standing feud; *Ghosts and Legends of Northumbria* says that Ridley was the name of his clan. Tegner calls him simply 'a young gallant of doubtful lineage'. The place of the ambush was supposedly a ravine called Pinkyn Cleugh. The ghostly procession is said still to haunt the area on the anniversary of the tragedy.

Northumberland has a rich heritage of ghost stories, most of them merely anecdotes and records of sightings. This tale is one of the most developed and is typical of the world wide belief in ghosts as 'spirits of the troubled dead'.

THE MAGIC OINTMENT

Grice: *Folk Tales of the North Country*
Keightley: *The Fairy Mythology*
Ghosts and Legends of Northumbria

The story of a couple or a woman chosen by the fairies to look after their baby is very common in folk tales about 'the Little People' throughout Britain. Equally so is the motif of a magic ointment for rubbing into the fairy baby's eyes, which is stolen by its human carers - who are then punished by blindness. In an alternative form of the story, set at Elsdon, a woman is abducted by a male fairy (sometimes the fairy king), who takes her into Fairyland where his wife is having a baby. The woman must act as midwife and nurse. At first she cannot see Fairyland in its true form; but this is rectified when she secretly steals some of the baby's magic ointment for her own eyes. Eventually she is rewarded with gold before returning home.

Keightley, writing in the late 19th Century, said that many Northumberland people still believed in fairies and cited a number of instances of people who claimed to have seen them. He also described a fairy-ring that could be found a few miles from Alnwick.

THE SLEEPING KING

Grice: *Folk Tales of the North Country*
Ghosts and Legends of Northumbria

The ancient castle in which the shepherd found himself is said to be the ruin at Sewingshields, which lies just to the east of Housesteads along Hadrian's Wall.

This type of plot - the 'sleeping king story'- is common in folk tales throughout Britain. The legend of King Arthur tells how, after being mortally wounded in his final battle, Arthur was taken away to be healed in the enchanted land of Avalon. Now he is resting in a secret hiding place in a hill or mountain, waiting for the call to come and rule again in all his former glory. The sleeping king in Scottish and Welsh tales may be either Arthur or one of their own national heroes.

Folk tale characters who find their way into enchanted realms are invariably haunted by the experience for the rest of their lives, and constantly but unsuccessfully seek to return there.

A similar tale, also once well known in Northumberland, is *Sir Guy the Seeker*. It tells of a gallant knight who finds his way into the subterranean regions below the ruins of Dunstanburgh Castle, which still stand on the coast, just north of Craster. There an extraordinarily tall old man invites him to take up the challenge that lies within. Behind a brass door he finds a hundred black marble horses and a hundred white marble knights all sleeping on the ground. Beyond them stands a crystal tomb guarded by skeletons, in which lies a beautiful lady, enchanted by the wizard Merlin to sleep until a knight can overcome the spell. Offered the choice of sword or horn, Sir Guy blows the horn. This causes the sleepers only to stir before falling back into unconsciousness. Pale red and yellow quartz, found in the rocks at Dunstanburgh, is said to be part of a treasure due to anyone who can successfully break the spell: they are known as 'Dunstanburgh diamonds'.

COMPLETE LIST OF SOURCES

Balfour, M C: *County Folklore Vol. IV: Northumberland* (London: David Nutt for the Folk Lore Society 1904)

Bosanquet, Rosalie E (Ed.): *In the Troublesome Times - The Cambo Women's Institute Book of 1922* (Newcastle-upon-Tyne: Northumberland Press 1929)

Briggs, Katherine M: *A Dictionary of British Folk-Tales in the English Language incorporating the F. J. Norton Collection Parts A and B* (London: Routledge & Kegan Paul, 1970, 1971)

Grice, F: *Folk Tales of the North Country drawn from Northumberland and Durham* (London & Edinburgh: Thomas Nelson & Sons 1944)

Henderson, William: *Notes on the Folk-Lore of the Northern Counties of England and the Borders, with an Appendix of Household Stories by S. Baring-Gould* (1866, republished by EP Publishing 1973)

Keightley, Thomas: *The Fairy Mythology* (London: G. Bell 1878)

Leighton, Alexander (Ed.): *Wilson's Tales of the Borders and of Scotland, Historical, Traditionary and Imaginative* (Manchester: James Ainsworth undated, probably c. 1840)

Service, James: *Metrical Legends of Northumberland* (Alnwick: W. Davison 1834)

Tegner, H: *Ghosts of the North Country* (Frank Graham 1974; Rothbury: Butler Publishing 1991)

Tongue, Ruth L: *Forgotten Folk-tales of the English Counties* (London: Routledge & Kegan Paul 1970)

Tynedale, Margaret: *County Legend & Folk-Lore: Old Northumbria* (London: Collins 1932)

Ghosts and Legends of Northumbria (Alnwick: Coquet Editions 1989)

Myth and Magic of Northumbria (Warkworth: Sandhill Press 1992)

www.england-in-particular.com